Fingernail clippings
Snail slime
Eagle Screech
Crocodile Tears
Monkey Sneeze
Hippo Sweat
broken wishbones

Boo
Stew

This book is dedicated to my coauthors—my son Devin, a picky eater who enjoys peanut butter and turkey sandwiches, and my daughter Darith, who will gamely try almost anything.

—D. L. W.

For Isabel and Olivia.

—J. E.

Published by
PEACHTREE PUBLISHING COMPANY INC.
1700 Chattahoochee Avenue
Atlanta, Georgia 30318-2112
www.peachtree-online.com

Edited by Jonah Heller
Design and composition by Adela Pons

The illustrations were rendered in acrylic paint on paper. The Scares were created in ink, painted with compressed air on a separate piece of paper, and added to the paintings with Adobe Photoshop.

Printed in February 2021 by Leo Paper Group in China
10 9 8 7 6 5 4 3 2 1
First Edition
ISBN 978-1-68263-221-5

Cataloging-in-Publication Data is available from the Library of Congress.

Boo Stew

Written by
Donna L. Washington

Illustrated by
Jeffrey Ebbeler

PEACHTREE
ATLANTA

CAFÉ

There were always Scares in Toadsuck Swamp, but Curly Locks didn't pay 'em much mind. The Scares kept to themselves. They only woke up at night, and the most annoyin' thing about 'em was their hootin' and hollerin'.

The only thing Curly Locks truly cared about was cookin'.

Sadly, the townsfolk ran the other way when she offered 'em batwing brownies, cat hair cupcakes, or toad eye toffees.

It was disappointin', but her momma just said "Do what your heart loves!" Well, her heart loved to cook!

One night, Curly Locks left a pan of lizard skin lasagna coolin' on the windowsill. When she returned, the dish was licked clean!

She peered out into Toadsuck. "Somebody out there likes my cookin'!"

The next mornin', the mayor was singin' to himself as he sat down to breakfast when an itty-bitty Scare opened the window and plopped right into the middle of his pancakes! It waggled its hairy little head.

"Gitchey Boo,
Gitchey Bon!
Gitchey Goo,
Gitchey Gone!"
MAYOR

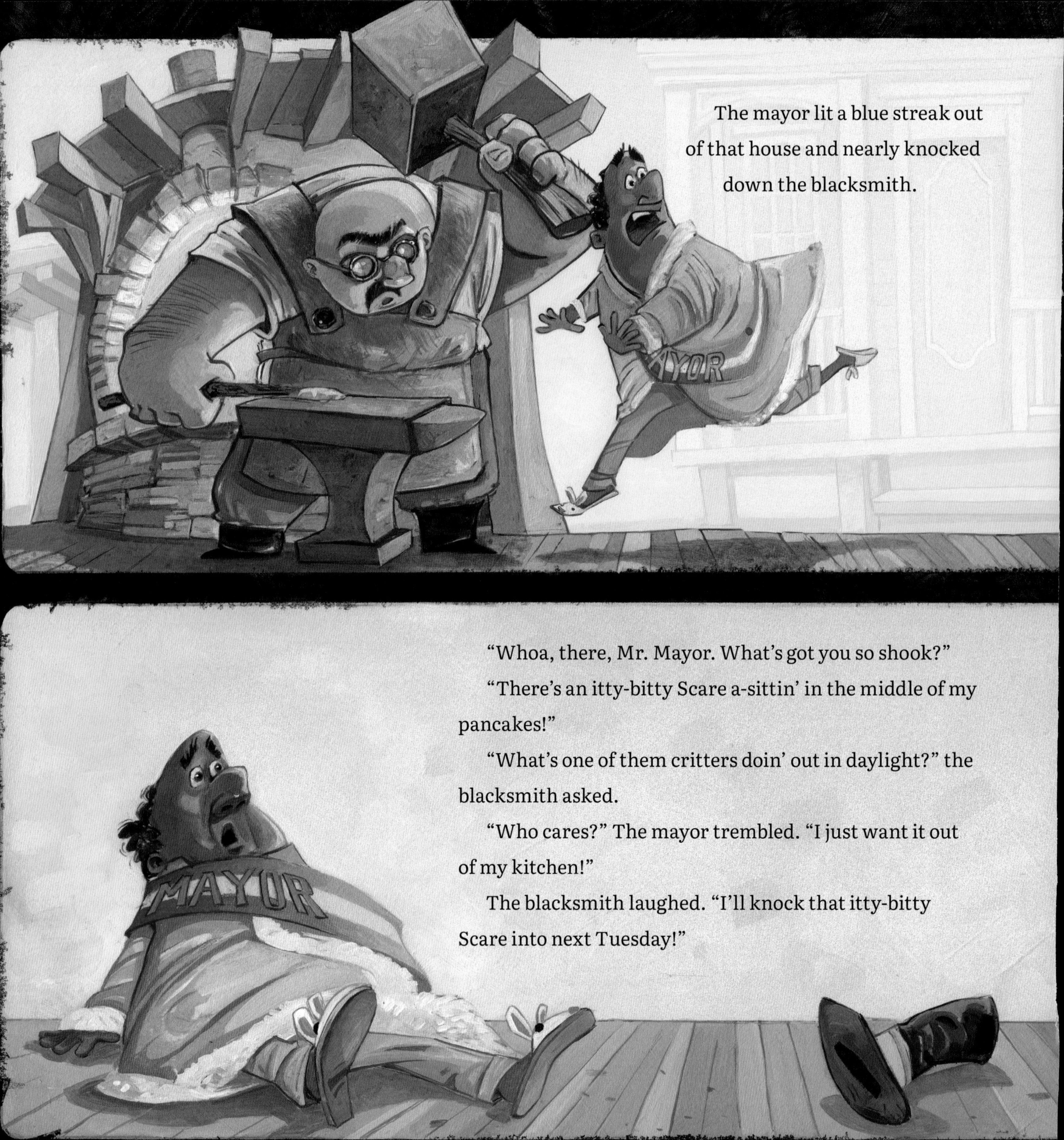

The mayor lit a blue streak out of that house and nearly knocked down the blacksmith.

"Whoa, there, Mr. Mayor. What's got you so shook?"

"There's an itty-bitty Scare a-sittin' in the middle of my pancakes!"

"What's one of them critters doin' out in daylight?" the blacksmith asked.

"Who cares?" The mayor trembled. "I just want it out of my kitchen!"

The blacksmith laughed. "I'll knock that itty-bitty Scare into next Tuesday!"

"I wouldn't go in there if I was you!" the mayor whispered.

"Well, you ain't me."

The blacksmith stuck out his chest and strutted into the mayor's house.

The itty-bitty Scare was sittin' in the middle of a big ol' mess on the mayor's table.

The blacksmith was gettin' ready to snatch that critter up by his ear when he felt a *tap, tap, tappin'* on his shoulder.

"Gitchey Boo,
Gitchey Goo,
Gitchey Bon!
Gitchey Gone!"

The blacksmith cut out of that house and ran smack-dab into the chicken rancher.

"Why y'all makin' such a fuss over one little Scare?" asked the chicken rancher.

"Because it's in my kitchen!" the mayor snapped.

"T-two Scares," stammered the blacksmith. "The s-s-second is bigger than the f-f-first!"

"Bah!" said the chicken rancher. "All they ever do is hoot and holler! Don't you fret none. I'll handle it!"

"I wouldn't go in there if I was you!" warned the blacksmith.

"Well, you ain't me."

The chicken rancher lifted his chin and swaggered into the mayor's house.

Lickety-split, that chicken rancher snatched the itty-bitty Scare by a tuft of hair and lassoed the other with his rope.

"You Scares don't scare me!" he roared.

The house started a-shakin'.

The rancher's knees started a-quakin'.

Thump! Thump! Whomp!
Thump! Thump! Whomp!
"Gitchey Boo, Gitchey Bon!
Gitchey Goo, Gitchey Gone!"

The chicken rancher nearly flew out of that house.

"There's three of 'em!" he hollered. "The last one's huge!"

Stories about the Scares spread like a kerosene fire.

Curly Locks was headin' into town when she saw folks runnin' through the streets.

"Where y'all goin'?" she yelled.

"There's Scares wreckin' the mayor's kitchen!" the dressmaker hollered back.

Curly Locks remembered the lizard skin lasagna that was licked clean from her windowsill. *Hmmm*, she thought. *I bet nobody's tried cookin' for 'em. I better get over there right away!*

A frightful din was comin' out of the mayor's house when Curly Locks arrived.

"Easy there, little lady!" the mayor called.

"There's three Scares in there!" the blacksmith added.

"I hear 'em," Curly Locks replied. "I'm gonna make 'em somethin' to eat."

"Bless your heart," said the innkeeper, "that don't sound like a good idea."

"Maybe it is!" the barber exclaimed. "Her cookin' could drive anything away."

Curly Locks walked up the front steps. "I wouldn't go in there if I was you!" yelled the chicken rancher.

"Well, you ain't me!"

And with that, Curly Locks clutched her basket, squared her shoulders, and marched into the house.

The door shut behind her, and the Scares got quiet. Curly Locks peeked into the kitchen. It was a frightful mess. She put her big-bellied pot on the potbellied stove, took out possum grease and toadstool, and set to work.

The cupboard burst open and an itty-bitty Scare jumped out.

Curly Locks didn't bat an eye. "I'll go if you like, but if I do, you'll never get a taste of my famous Boo Stew."

"Boo Stew? OOOOOOOOOH!" The itty-bitty Scare sat down at the table and banged his bowl and spoon together.

"Ah, ah, ah," said Curly Locks. "First, we clean off the table, then we wash our hands."

Curly Locks was adding powdered beetle and lizard spit to the pot…when she felt a *tap, tap, tappin'* on her shoulder.

Curly Locks stiffened but didn't let on that she was startled. "I'll go if you like, but if I do, you'll never get a taste of my famous Boo Stew."

"Boo Stew? OOOOOOOOOOH!" The middling Scare clapped his scaly hands.

"Clean the floor first," said Curly Locks, "then set the table."

Curly Locks added moose ear broth, toenail clippings, and gnat juice.

Thump! Thump! Whomp!
Thump! Thump! Whomp!

The biggest, thumpiest, whompiest Scare of all came a-gnashin' his Scare teeth, a-wagglin' his Scare claws, and a-clompin' his Scare feet!

Curly Locks gripped her spoon so tight it nearly snapped in two. "I'll go if you like, but if I do, you'll never get a taste of my famous Boo Stew."

"Boo Stew? OOOOOOOOOH!"

That big Scare licked his jowls in anticipation.

"Clean the ceiling, please."

By the time the kitchen was put right, the stew was pipin' hot and ready to eat! Curly Locks took a taste and smiled.

"I hope y'all are hungry, 'cause this might just be the best batch of Boo Stew east of the Mississippi."

Those Scares ate until they were full
as ticks in high summer.
They licked their fingers.
They licked their toes.
They licked each other's toes!

Curly Locks didn't mind their sorry manners. Why, she'd never seen a single soul enjoy her cookin' so!

"Carry yourselves on back to Toadsuck Swamp," cooed Curly Locks, "and I'll make Boo Stew and lots of other things for you—and your friends—every night!"

Some say that was the finest deal ever struck in those parts.

The Scares got themselves a heap of delicious food. With their bellies full, they didn't spend all night hootin' and hollerin'.

The townsfolk got plenty of sleep now that Toadsuck was quiet.

The mayor got a fine tale to tell for years to come.

And Curly Locks...?

She got a load of hearty eaters
who appreciated her cookin'.
That was the best thing of all.

Venus Flytrap Drool
Dandruff
Belly Button Lint
Stinky Cheese
Runny Cheese
Moldy Cheese
eel-lectricity